Herman the Helper

BY ROBERT KRAUS

PICTURES BY
JOSE ARUEGO & ARIANE DEWEY

Aladdin Paperbacks

Don't worry, I'll help you.

Aladdin Paperbacks
An imprint of Simon & Schuster
Children's Publishing Division
1230 Avenue of the Americas
New York, NY 10020

15 14 13

Originally published by Windmill Books, Inc.
Printed in Hong Kong

Library of Congress Cataloging-in-Publication Data
Kraus, Robert, 1925-
Herman the helper/by Robert Kraus; pictures by Jose Aruego & Ariane Dewey.
p. cm.
Reprint. Originally published: New York: Windmill Books, 1974.
Summary: Herman the helpful octopus is always willing to assist
anyone who needs his help—old or young, friend or enemy.
ISBN 0-671-66270-8 pbk
[1. Octopus—Fiction. 2. Brotherliness—Fiction. 3. Helpfulness—
Fiction.] I. Aruego, Jose, ill. II. Dewey, Ariane, ill.
III. Title.
[PZ7.K868HF 1987] 87-32071
[E]—dc19 CIP AC

For Pamela, Bruce, Billy & Juan

Herman liked to help.

He helped his mother.

I'll plant it here.
Beautiful.

He helped his father.

That's my dad.

He helped his brothers and sisters.

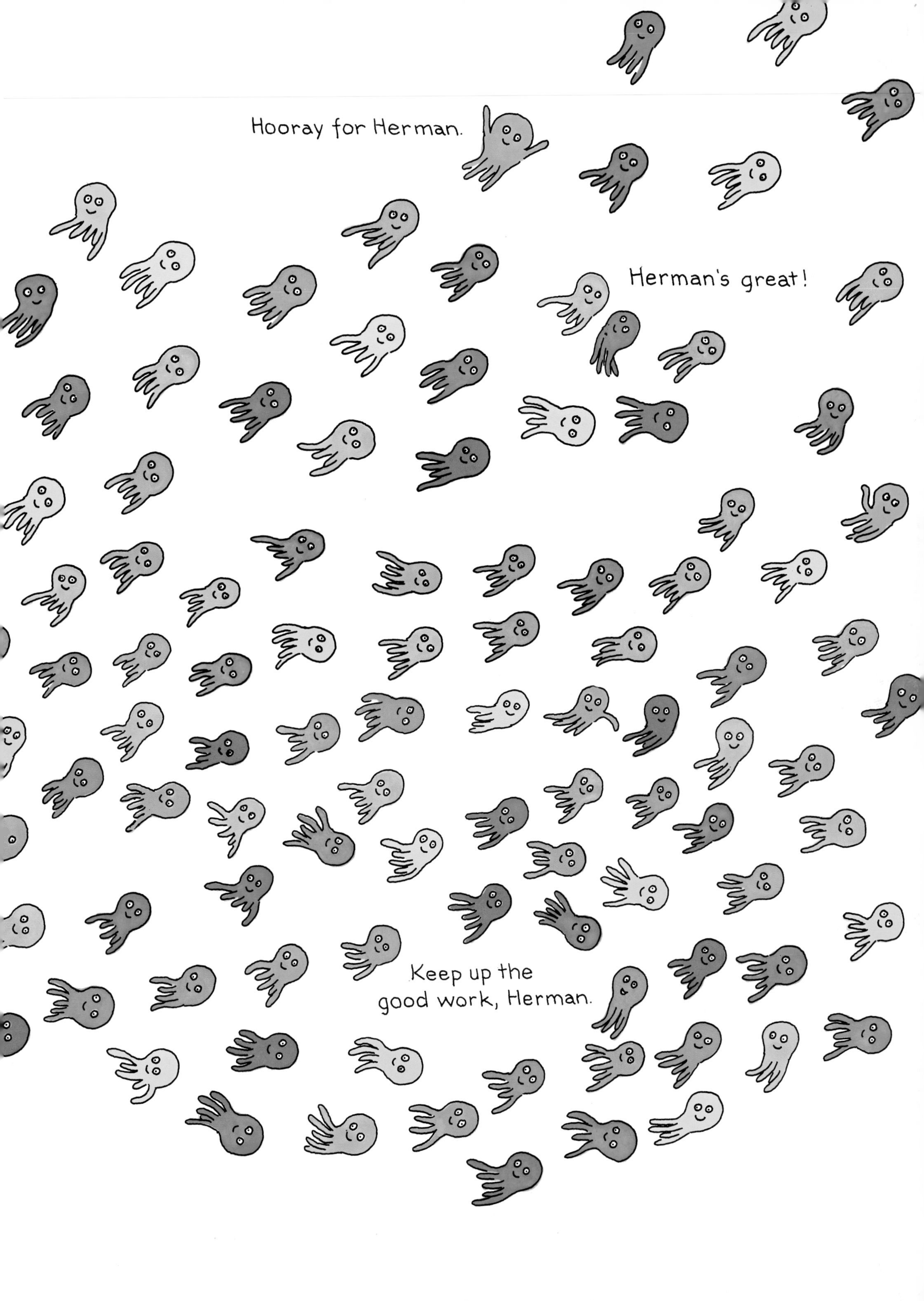
Hooray for Herman.
Herman's great!
Keep up the
good work, Herman.

He helped his aunt.

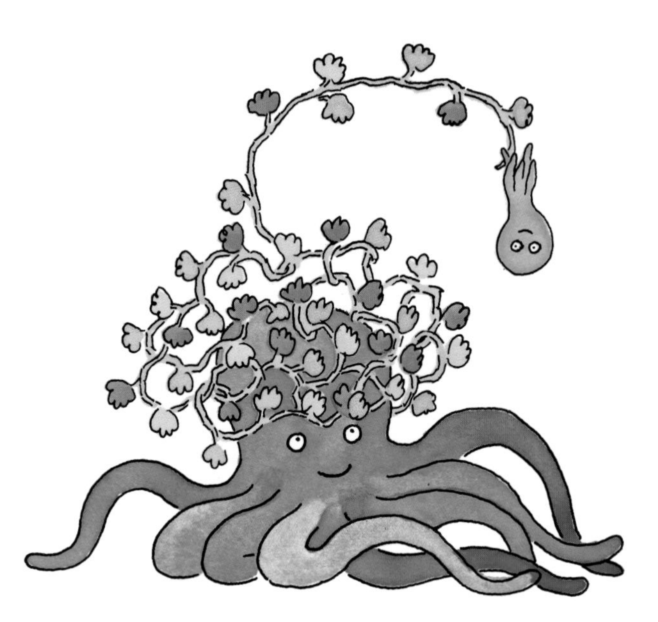

What a beautiful
bonnet, Herman.

Yes.

He helped his uncle.

He helped his friends.

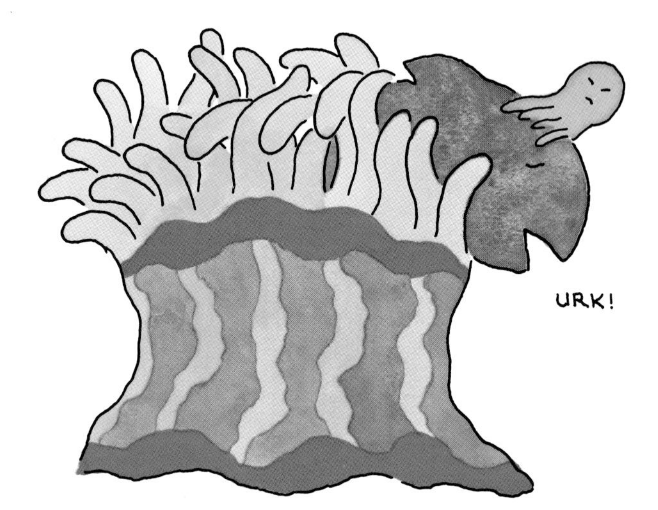

Many thanks, Herman.

He helped his enemies.
Okay.
Help! It's after us!
I'll camouflage you with my ink.

SISSSSSSSSS
Herman saved the day!

He helped the young.

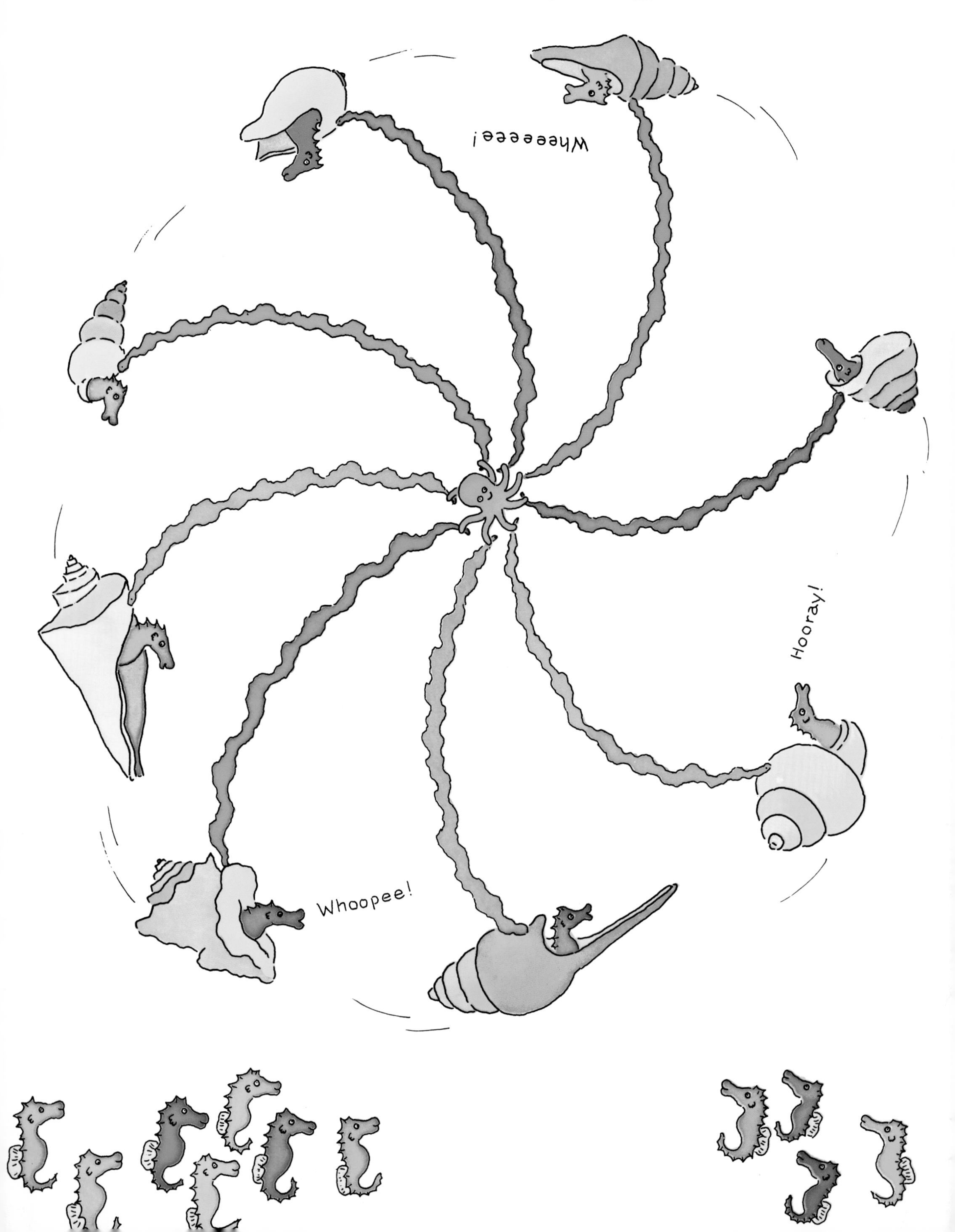

He helped the old.

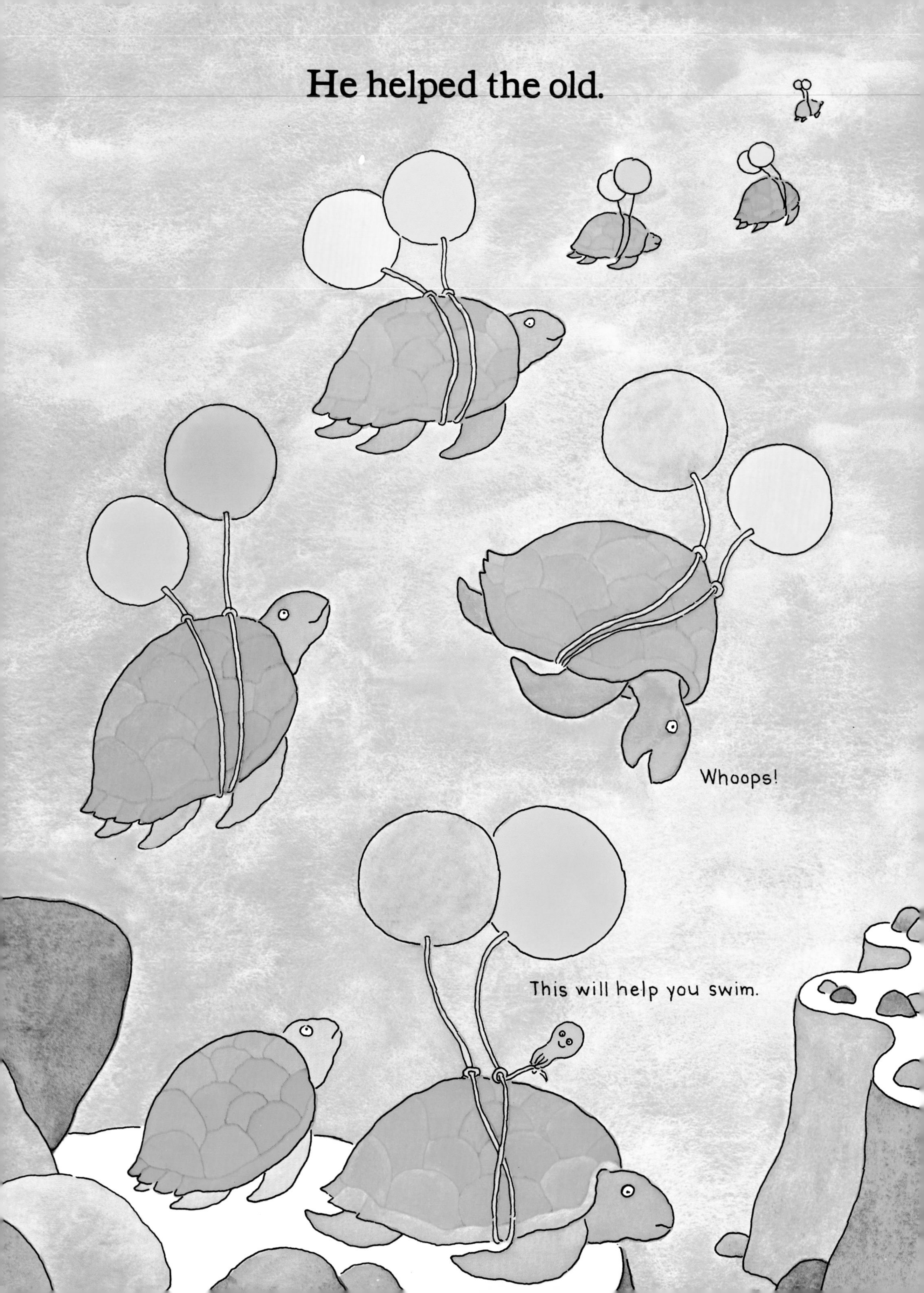

He helped the poor and needy.

What a helper!
Bless you, Herman.

He helped the fireman.

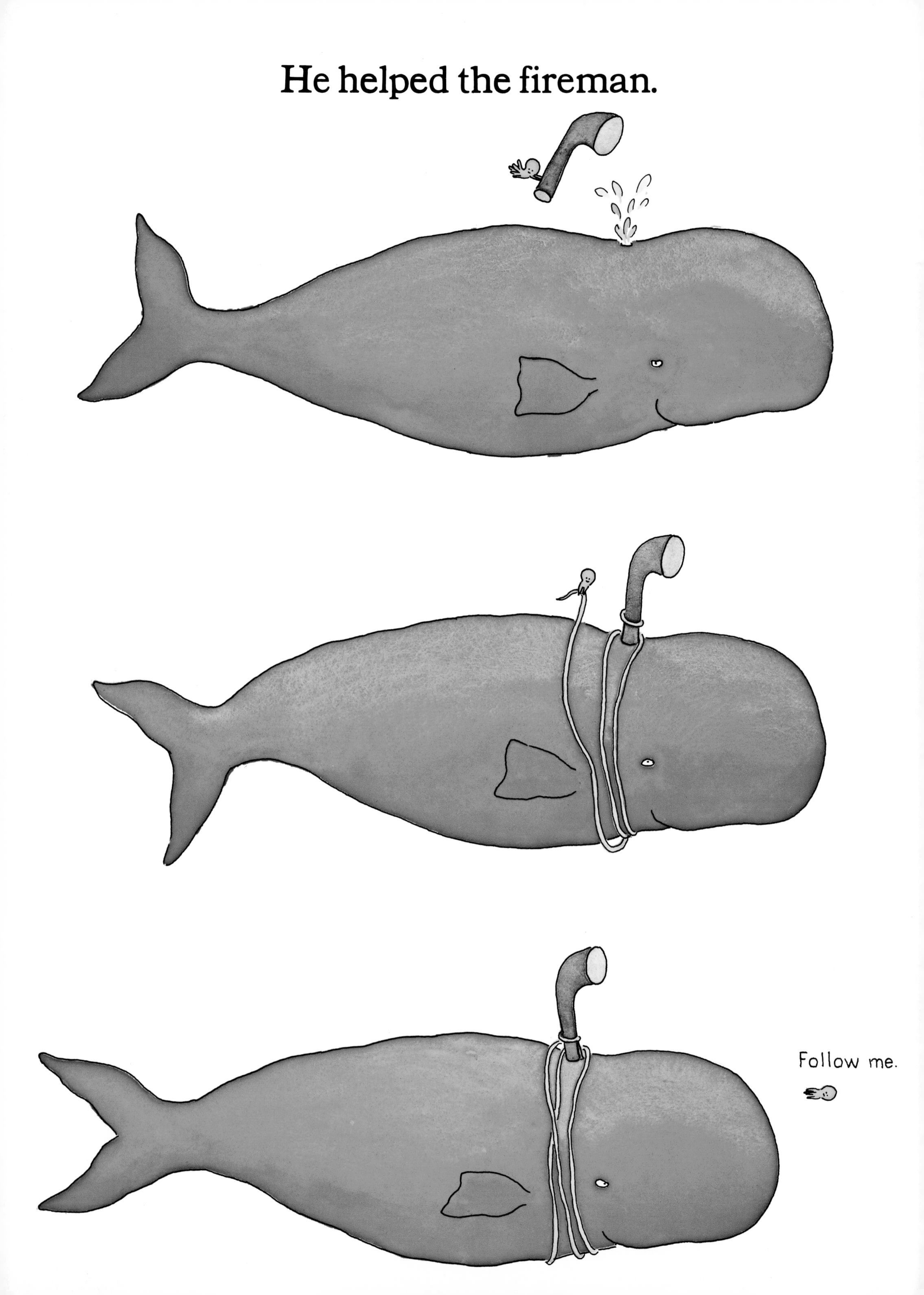

Hose it down, Chief!
Okay, Herm.

He helped the policeman.

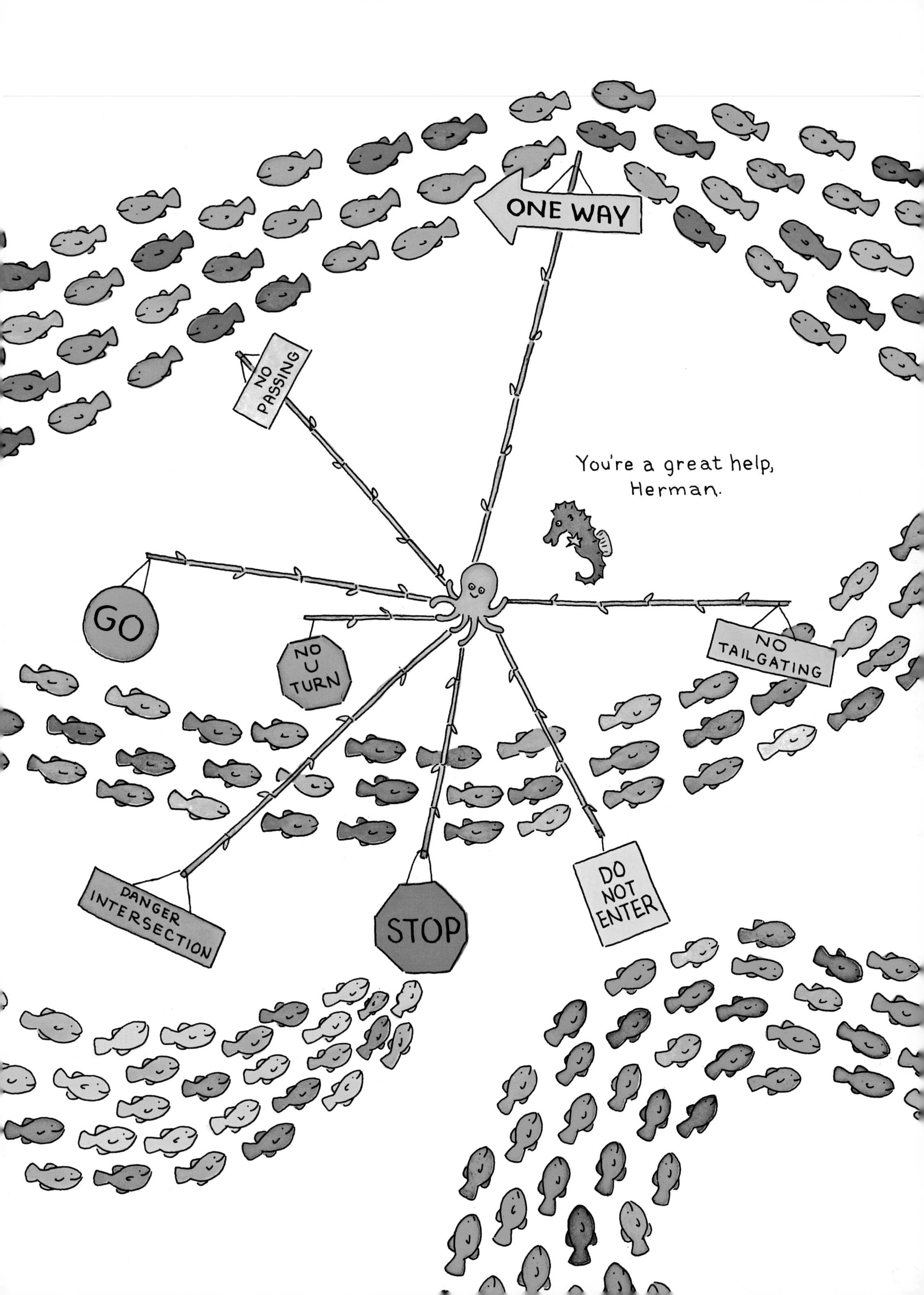

ONE WAY
NO PASSING
You're a great help, Herman.
GO
NO U TURN
NO TAILGATING
DANGER INTERSECTION
STOP
DO NOT ENTER

Then the clock struck six
and Herman hurried home.

Six o'clock already?

He washed his hands and face.

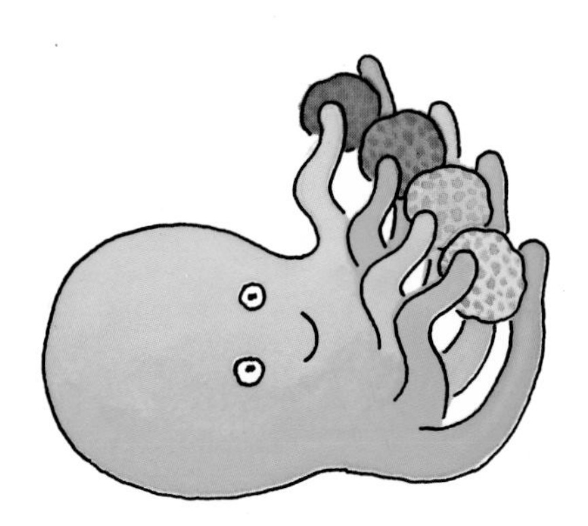

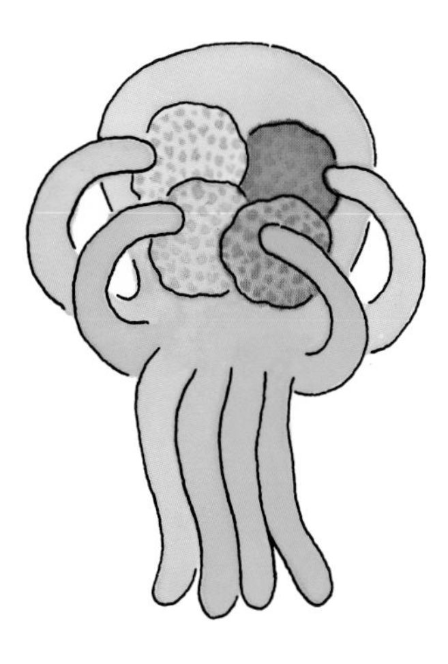

I'm hungry!

And sat down to supper.

"May I help you to some mashed potatoes?"
asked Herman's father.

"No thanks,"
said Herman,
"I'll help myself."